THE KID NEXT DOOR
AND OTHER HEADACHES

The Kid Next Door
and Other Headaches

Stories About Adam Joshua

by Janice Lee Smith

drawings by Dick Gackenbach

HarperCollins*Publishers*

The Kid Next Door and other Headaches:
Stories about Adam Joshua
Text copyright © 1984 by Janice Lee Smith
Illustrations copyright © 1984 by Dick Gackenbach
All rights reserved. No part of this book may be
used or reproduced in any manner whatsoever without
written permission except in the case of brief quotations
embodied in critical articles and reviews. Printed in
the United States of America. For information address
HarperCollins Children's Books, a division of
HarperCollins Publishers, 10 East 53rd Street,
New York, N.Y. 10022.

Library of Congress Cataloging in Publication Data
Smith, Janice Lee, 1949–
    The kid next door and other headaches.

    Summary: In a series of episodes, two young boys who
are best friends share different viewpoints about neatness,
the best kind of pet, super heroes, horrible cousins, and
what consideration an overnight guest is entitled to.
    [1. Friendship—Fiction] I. Gackenbach, Dick, ill.
II. Title.
PZ7.S6499Ki   1984   [E]   83-47689
ISBN 0-06-025792-X
ISBN 0-06-025793-8 (lib. bdg.)

For my parents, Jim and Olivia—
who know all about raising eccentric,
exasperating youngsters (my brothers!)—
with love and thanks!

Contents

THE KID NEXT DOOR
AND OTHER HEADACHES

The Kid Next Door

If you were trapped in an earthquake and you needed somebody big to rescue you, somebody strong, somebody who knew what to do—you wouldn't call Nelson.

And if you were ever in a horrible battle and you needed someone who was brave in battles, and brave about bullies, and helped you be brave about those things too—you wouldn't even think of Nelson.

But if you didn't need a hero, but needed a friend—someone who would listen when he

3

should, and would understand when he could, and would like you no matter what—then Nelson is who you'd choose. Every time.

At least that's what Adam Joshua had always thought.

But then one day Nelson said, "Adam Joshua, just look at this tree house!"

Adam Joshua looked. He thought the tree house looked fine.

"It looks great, Nelson," he said. "Couldn't be better."

"Couldn't be better?" Nelson said, kicking at a pile of space toys. "Couldn't be better?" he shouted, jumping on a stack of comic books.

"We're supposed to share the tree house," Nelson said, "but I can't even sit on my side of the tree house because of all your stuff."

"But Nelson," Adam Joshua said, getting up to move space toys and comics so that Nelson could sit, "some of these things are your things too. And some of these things are things you've given me. And," he said, "some are things we've collected together, and those are the things we share."

4

Nelson sat down, but he sat down on an old spring that Adam Joshua had found and carried up to the tree house that morning.

"I've had it!" Nelson yelled, jumping right up again and waving the spring. "I don't get mad very often, Adam Joshua. But now I'm mad!" Then Nelson yelled some really awful, no-good, and mostly not true things at Adam Joshua.

Adam Joshua couldn't believe Nelson would say those things. "That does it, Nelson!" yelled Adam Joshua. "I've had it too!" he shouted. "We're not best friends anymore!" he hollered.

"I already knew that," said Nelson. He turned his back on Adam Joshua, climbed down the tree house ladder, and walked away.

Adam Joshua was left standing there with a lot more to say and nobody to say it to. He tipped his head back and clenched his fists.

"AND I REALLY MEAN IT, NELSON!" he yelled.

Nobody answered.

"I MEAN REALLY!" he shouted. Then he

kicked stuff out of the way and sat down on the tree house floor to think.

When he saw a piece of chalk down by his foot, he stopped thinking, and stood up.

He drew a chalk line across the ceiling of the tree house. He drew lines on its walls. He kicked things out of the way and drew a line down the middle of the tree house floor.

"**YOURS**," he wrote on the wall on Nelson's half of the tree house. "**MINE!**" he wrote on his half, and then added a drawing of himself playing in their tree house all alone.

Adam Joshua shoved all the comic books and space toys to his side, and left the pine-cones, and rocks, and seashells on Nelson's. He drew a line straight down through the middle of the Superman poster.

"Fair's fair," he said.

Adam Joshua picked up their turtle. He patted it on the back, and gave it some food, and knocked on its shell to see if it was still in there.

Nelson had named the turtle Clyde. Adam Joshua always hated that name. Adam Joshua drew a line down the middle of the turtle's shell. "**CLYDE**," he wrote on the side that belonged to Nelson. "**IRVING**," he wrote on his side.

"You just be sure you come when I call," Adam Joshua told Clyde/Irving, knocking on his shell to say good-bye. Then he climbed down the tree house ladder, and drew a line down the middle of every step along the way.

———

In the kitchen, Adam Joshua stomped past his baby sister, Amanda Jane. She reached out a hand to pat him and handed him her teddy bear.

"Don't mess with me, Amanda Jane!" Adam Joshua shouted. "This is no time for bears!"

Up in his room, Adam Joshua looked out his window. From his window he could see through Nelson's window. Through Nelson's window he could see Nelson, standing beside his favorite bowl of fish. Nelson was pointing at Adam Joshua's house, and shaking his fist, and waving his arms. Adam Joshua used his

binoculars to see if Nelson's fish were agreeing with what Nelson had to say.

He opened his window and leaned out.

"Don't believe everything you hear!" he shouted.

Adam Joshua got a marker and pulled down the window shade. He stood between the window and the shade and wrote on the back of the shade.

"YOU'RE NOT EVEN MY WORST FRIEND, NELSON. YOU'RE JUST NO FRIEND AT ALL!"

Adam Joshua crawled out from behind the shade and sat down on the floor beside it to wait.

"That should do it," he said, after he'd waited long enough.

"THE SAME TO YOU, ADAM JOSHUA!" Nelson's shade said. **"NOBODY WOULD EVER WANT YOU FOR A FRIEND ANYWAY!"** Nelson's shade shouted.

"Yep, that did it," said Adam Joshua, putting his marker away.

Adam Joshua looked around his room. All around were things Nelson had given him, things Nelson had made for him, and things Nelson had helped him collect.

Adam Joshua got out an empty box and got busy.

He put Nelson's comics in the box, and Nelson's drawings, and Nelson's pictures of fish. He put in the green plastic pickle whistle Nelson had given him because he had two, and some of Nelson's baby teeth.

He took his bag of jelly beans down off the shelf.

Adam Joshua loved jelly beans, except black.

Nelson had given Adam Joshua jelly beans, with all the black picked out. Adam Joshua ate two and put the rest in the box.

He crawled under his bed and got the dried worm collection Nelson had helped him collect, and the space figure with a broken arm that Nelson let him have because it had a broken arm, and one of Nelson's old socks.

"**FOR NELSON,**" Adam Joshua wrote on the box, "**WHO USED TO BE MY FRIEND.**"

11

Then he dug down in the box and got another jelly bean, took the box outside, and pulled it up into the tree house he used to share with Nelson.

———————

Late that night, Adam Joshua could see Nelson lying in bed with his light still on, talking to his fish.

Adam Joshua lay all alone in the dark, talking to himself.

"He wasn't all that great as a friend to begin with," he said, rolling over and pounding his pillow with his fist to get it the way he liked it.

He lay back down and thought about things.

For one thing, he thought, Nelson liked stuff very neat. Adam Joshua hated stuff that way.

For a second thing, Nelson absolutely loved fish. Adam Joshua had never thought about them much before, but he thought he was starting to hate them.

Also, Nelson acted strange sometimes and then Adam Joshua didn't understand him at all. And sometimes Nelson acted like he didn't understand Adam Joshua either. Adam Joshua didn't think that was the way friends should be.

"So it's just as well it's over," he said, standing up and stomping on his pillow to get it more comfortable.

Still, Adam Joshua thought, lying down and burying his face in the pillow, he would like a friend. But he'd choose a friend more carefully next time. He'd choose somebody who would always understand him.

Except, Adam Joshua didn't always understand himself. "So it won't be easy," he muttered into the pillow.

It would be nice, he thought, if his new friend was someone who liked games the way Nelson used to, and liked jokes the way Nelson used to, and even liked messes. In fact, his new friend might turn out to be a messy person himself.

And as long as his new friend was going to be perfect, Adam Joshua thought he'd also like him to be strong, and brave, and good in emergencies.

He turned around and put his head on the foot of the bed and his feet on the pillow.

"Superman would be just right," he said, falling asleep.

———

The first thing after breakfast the next morning, Adam Joshua went for a walk to see if he could find somebody new.

On one end of his block was a kid named Jody. Adam Joshua thought he liked Jody, but he'd never had much time to play with her. Now he had a lot of time.

Adam Joshua could hear Jody laughing before he got to her backyard. He crept along the side of her house and peeked around the corner.

Nelson was standing there, looking terrible, and Jody was standing there laughing at Nelson.

"Fish!" Jody said, laughing. "Fish! Nelson, I don't understand. Nobody could be as crazy about fish as you are."

Adam Joshua knew how Jody felt, but he didn't think it was any reason for Jody to make Nelson feel bad.

"Nelson," Jody said, laughing so hard she had to hold her sides, "that's the funniest thing I ever heard."

Adam Joshua didn't think he liked Jody much after all. He turned around and crept away again.

At the other end of the block was a kid named Frank. Adam Joshua had never liked Frank, but he thought maybe he could get used to him.

"But we have to play by my rules," Frank said after Adam Joshua got there. "Because in my yard you have to do what I say."

Frank had rules Adam Joshua had never even heard of.

"I don't think this is the way you play checkers," Adam Joshua said, watching Frank. "When Nelson and I play we each get turns."

"Out!" yelled Frank, jumping up and scattering checkers everywhere. "And stay out!" he shouted after Adam Joshua, and he threw the checker board after him too.

Adam Joshua went home to play checkers by himself.

"But just until Superman gets here," he said.

———

Later, Adam Joshua crawled up the tree house ladder to see if his box for Nelson was gone. It was, but a new box said: "**FOR ADAM JOSHUA.**"

Adam Joshua opened it up in his bedroom. Inside were his records, and his no-nosed elephant, and a stuffed cloth chicken with the tail missing.

When Adam Joshua's kaleidoscope broke, he gave Nelson all the pieces so that Nelson could build something new. All the pieces were in the box.

When Adam Joshua heard that Nelson had the measles and the measles were awful, Adam Joshua sent him one flat blue football, three marbles, four carrot tops, an avocado seed, and a poster of the fish of northern Minnesota so that Nelson could have things to think about.

Nelson sent them all back in the box.

Not long ago, Adam Joshua let Nelson borrow his one-eyed, one-armed, no-legged teddy bear to show that Nelson was the best friend he'd ever had.

"**NOT ANYMORE!**" the note on the bear said.

"I can't believe it," said Adam Joshua, tipping the box over and shaking it to see if anything else was there.

The sock fell out with a note pinned to it.

"**YOURS**," said the note.

———

Amanda Jane went crawling along the hall and poked her head into Adam Joshua's room.

"Well, hi," Adam Joshua said, going over and picking her up and kissing her. "You're not much," he said, "but you're going to have to do."

Adam Joshua took his best sister, Amanda Jane, outside, and he threw Nelson's sock over the hedge between their yards.

Then Adam Joshua tried to teach Amanda Jane to play space spies, and he tried to teach her to play soccer, and he tried to teach her to catch.

Amanda Jane put the heads of the space spies in her mouth, and she licked the soccer ball, and when Adam Joshua threw a ball for her to catch, it hit her on the head.

"Oh, Amanda Jane," Adam Joshua said, kissing her head on the sore spot. He sat down to play "Where's the Baby?" with her because that was the only game she knew.

Adam Joshua would put his hands over his eyes, and Amanda Jane would put her hands over her eyes, and then Adam Joshua would look up fast, and then Amanda Jane would look up fast, and then Adam Joshua would yell, "BOO!" and Amanda Jane would fall over giggling.

Adam Joshua sighed. If Superman didn't show up he was going to be spending the rest of his life playing "Where's the Baby?" with Amanda Jane and never getting to play soccer, or space spies, or checkers, or much of anything else ever again.

Adam Joshua could hear Nelson playing with his own baby, Henry, on the other side of the hedge.

"That's not the way to do it!" Adam Joshua heard Nelson yell at Henry. "Don't you know anything?" Adam Joshua heard Henry start to cry.

Adam Joshua tickled Amanda Jane to make her laugh out loud.

Nelson's head popped up over the top of the hedge.

Amanda Jane waved at Nelson.

"Amanda Jane," Adam Joshua hollered, grabbing her hand down again. "Don't you know the enemy when you see him?" he said.

Adam Joshua played "Where's the Baby?" six more times with Amanda Jane. Then he lay down under a tree to rest. When he opened his eyes Amanda Jane was gone.

"Amanda Jane!" he shouted.

He saw two legs and two arms and one head and all the rest of Amanda Jane come backwards through the hedge.

"**KEEP THIS BABY QUIET!**" Adam Joshua read on the bottom of Amanda Jane's disposable diaper. "**OTHER PEOPLE ARE PLAYING!**"

Adam Joshua took his marker out of his pocket, and he crawled over by the hedge and

waited until he could see Henry's foot. He gently pulled on the foot until the rest of Henry came too.

"**DON'T MAKE THIS BABY CRY**," Adam Joshua wrote on Henry's plastic diaper. "**OR ANYBODY EJSE!**" He gave Henry a kiss and carefully put him back through the hedge.

Adam Joshua lay under the tree and waited.

Amanda Jane disappeared.

Adam Joshua lay under the tree and waited.

Amanda Jane came back through the hedge.

Adam Joshua went over and picked up Amanda Jane and looked at her diaper.

The sock was pinned to it.

"Figures," said Adam Joshua. He took Amanda Jane and the sock inside.

———

Later Adam Joshua tried playing space spies outside by himself.

It wasn't easy being the hero spy and the enemy spy both at the same time.

"ZAM, ZAP! ZOW, ZING!" Adam Joshua yelled, zowing, and zinging, and zapping the enemy.

"Ow, augh!" Adam Joshua yelled, running around to be the enemy just as he got hit, and falling down on the ground fast, and dying a long, slow, death.

Sometimes, when he was being the hero, Adam Joshua called himself Steel, and sometimes he called himself Rock, and sometimes he called himself Eagle.

But the enemy spy was named Nelson every time.

Adam Joshua heard noises coming from the other side of Nelson's hedge. It sounded like a stampede.

Adam Joshua dropped to his stomach and

looked through a hole in the hedge.

Henry was gone, and Nelson was playing a game that he and Adam Joshua always played together. It was a game with a good guy and a bad guy and a lot of noise. Nelson was running from one side of the yard to the other, being the good guy and the bad guy, and making noise for both of them.

"Take that, Adam Joshua!" Nelson yelled, being the good guy.

"Augh," Nelson said, running over to lie on the ground with his hands on his throat and his feet in the air. "You were just too smart for me, Nelson," Nelson said.

Adam Joshua didn't think Nelson's game was the least bit funny. He crawled backwards on his stomach, and stomped into the house and up to his room.

Adam Joshua sat on his bed looking at his stuff on the floor. There wasn't anything to do. He thought there might be something to do if he thought about it, but he didn't feel much like thinking about it. He stared out the window.

All of a sudden he saw Nelson come into his own room and go over to lie on the bed.

Nelson lay on his stomach with his head in the pillow. Sometimes he'd raise his head up, and then he'd bury it in the pillow again.

Adam Joshua got his binoculars.

Nelson was crying. Nelson never cried. "Unless he feels just terrible," Adam Joshua said, watching.

And he stood watching Nelson for a long time.

———

Adam Joshua went downstairs to the kitchen, and past his mother, who was feeding Amanda

Jane. He dug in the kitchen closet and came out with a broom, and a dustpan, and a garbage bag.

"That's a great idea," his mother said, watching him. "And I'll be up to your room to help you just as soon as I've finished here."

Adam Joshua glared at his mother, and he hauled everything out the back door, and dragged it all up the tree house ladder.

He held one side of the garbage bag open with his foot, and the other side open with a rock. He threw in paper cups he'd mixed paint in, and a Frisbee he'd cut the middle out of, and orange peels he'd been saving.

"Don't worry," he said, knocking on Clyde/Irving's shell. "You can come out now. You get to stay."

Adam Joshua threw shells and rocks he didn't like in the garbage bag, and a bird's nest that had fallen from the tree, and all the yarn that had once made up a Christmas stocking. He shoved what wouldn't fit in the bag over into the corner, and he swept up the rest.

"All clear now," he said, rapping on Clyde/Irving's shell. Adam Joshua dropped the garbage bag down from the tree house. He dragged it into the house and up the stairs. He opened the bag and took out the yarn and bird's nest. Then he sat on the bag until it got smaller, and he shoved it under his bed.

———

When Adam Joshua got back out to the tree house, Nelson's side was a mess. There were books about fish tossed neatly around, and

piles of rocks placed neatly around, and drawings and pictures, and stuff stacked neatly everywhere. It wasn't as good a mess as Adam Joshua could have made, but for Nelson it was fine.

There was a small bag on Adam Joshua's side of the tree house. Adam Joshua opened it up. Inside were five jelly beans, two yellow, a red, a green, and one black.

"Must still be mad," said Adam Joshua, picking out the four good jelly beans and putting the black one over on Nelson's side.

"He's like that," said Adam Joshua. He pulled the sock out of his pocket, and folded it neatly, and put it on Nelson's side, under the jelly bean. Then he sat in the tree house, reading comics and waiting for Nelson to come along.

A Dog Named George

Adam Joshua had space ships, and sailing ships, and fishing poles, and half a turtle.

What he didn't have was a dog.

Adam Joshua had stuffed elephants without noses, and stuffed chickens without tails, and a baby sister who had never been his idea to begin with.

What he really wanted was a dog.

"Just a little one," Adam Joshua told his mother and his father. "He wouldn't be any trouble because I'd take care of him. You'd never even notice he was around."

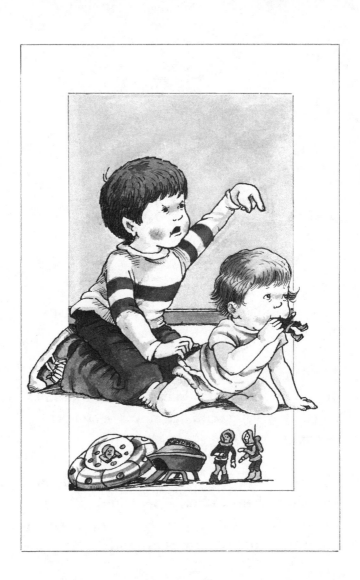

"Well, I love dogs," said his father. "But when I was your age I found out that even a little dog can be a big responsibility."

"But he'd be my friend," said Adam Joshua. "And he'd be the best dog there ever was."

"A dog is still a lot of work," said Adam Joshua's mother. "And after the fun's worn off it can be a lot of bother. We're going to have to think about it."

Amanda Jane went crawling by with one of Adam Joshua's Armand's Legion of Space Spies sticking out of her mouth.

"You had this baby without thinking about it," Adam Joshua yelled as he went crawling right along behind her to get it back. He showed his parents the broken space spy.

"And she's more trouble than a dog ever could be," he muttered, going to his room, and taking his broken spy along with him to see if he could fix it.

———

Each night, Adam Joshua would lie all alone in the dark and watch Nelson with his light still on, talking to his fish.

Each night, Adam Joshua would lie all alone in bed and think about talking to his dog whenever he got to get him.

There were a lot of nights like that.

Some nights he thought about getting a big dog, brown, big enough to ride on in case he wanted to, and big enough to rescue people in case it needed to, and big enough to scare scary things away, just in case.

He'd call him George.

Some nights Adam Joshua thought about getting a beautiful dog, white, with a lot of hair, beautiful enough to win blue ribbons at dog shows, and beautiful enough to get her picture in the newspapers, and smart enough to learn all the tricks there were.

He'd call her George.

But most nights, Adam Joshua thought about getting a dog that wasn't too big, and wasn't too beautiful, but who would know when to play, and would know when to listen, and would know enough to learn most of the tricks that Adam Joshua would know how to teach him.

Adam Joshua had a picture in his room that

his great-aunt Emily had given him. It was a picture of how she used to be when she was a little girl growing up in Kansas, and in the picture was a dog that had grown up in Kansas too.

"He wasn't very big," Great-Aunt Emily told him, "and he wasn't very handsome, but he was a good friend, and he saved my life one day."

Adam Joshua looked at the picture all the time, just so he could look at the dog.

"We were running together on the prairie," Great-Aunt Emily told Adam Joshua, "and I was picking wild flowers. I had put out my hand for some when my dog started barking to warn me, and he grabbed my sleeve and pulled my hand away.

"It was a rattlesnake," Great-Aunt Emily said. "It was lying behind some buffalo bones where I couldn't see it. It was lying right where I was going to put my hand."

Adam Joshua would lie in bed thinking about the story, and then he'd lie in bed thinking about getting a dog just like that.

He didn't think he'd ever get to get him, but if he did he'd call him George.

———

Then one evening, when Adam Joshua's father walked in from work, a puppy walked in with him. The puppy was mostly ears, and mostly tummy, and mostly tongue, and had legs so short they were hardly there at all.

Adam Joshua recognized him right away.

"George!" he hollered.

———

George tugged at Adam Joshua's pant legs, and barked at his shoelaces. George pulled down Adam Joshua's socks, and climbed right up his leg and into his arms to lick his face and say, "Hi!"

"Don't worry if you feel shy," Adam Joshua told George. "You'll feel at home here in no time."

George galloped around the living room, and tripped over his feet, and tumbled over his ears, and slid around on his stomach. Adam Joshua galloped, and tumbled, and slid right along.

George lay on the floor to rest and pant. Adam Joshua lay on the floor to pant too. When he looked back up, George's ears were being eaten by Amanda Jane.

"Hey!" yelled Adam Joshua, going over and taking ears out of Amanda Jane's mouth and drying them off on his shirt. "Hey! You cut that out!" shouted Adam Joshua. "George will never like it here if he thinks you're going to be eating him all the time!"

———

"Time for bed," Adam Joshua told George.

"How about the garage?" asked his mother.

"How about the laundry room?" asked his father.

"You've got to be kidding," said Adam Joshua, getting the guest pillows and blanket, and heading for his room with George right behind him.

His mother followed behind George. "Hold it," she told them both.

Together Adam Joshua and his mother found an old pillow and made a soft cover for it. "And would this do?" his mother asked,

digging in a chest. "It was your favorite blanket when you were a baby," she said, holding up an old blue blanket with holes in the middle and chewed-up edges.

"Fred!" yelled Adam Joshua, grabbing his old blanket and curling up with it on the floor to see if it still worked.

"Still works fine," said Adam Joshua.

"George. This is Fred," Adam Joshua said. He curled the blanket up on the floor and the

39

GEORGE'S CORNER

puppy up on the blanket. George started chewing the edges.

"That's the idea," said Adam Joshua. "You've got it just right," he said.

———

"**GEORGE'S CORNER**," Adam Joshua wrote on the wall in his room above George's corner.

"That's your name," he said, showing George.

"This is your corner," Adam Joshua said, putting George there.

George didn't stay a minute.

George bounced across the room and into the closet and brought things down with a crash.

George used the cover on Adam Joshua's bed to climb on, and he climbed to the top of the bed, and fought with the pillow and fought with the cover, and fell off and scooted under the bed, and came out with a dirty shirt.

"I can't believe it," said Adam Joshua, kicking things back in the closet and throwing the shirt back under the bed.

The bottom dresser drawer was open, and George crawled in and snuggled down and bounced up again, ready to play. The third dresser drawer was open a little, and George put his nose in the crack and pulled at it until he could get the rest of the drawer open too. He jumped in, and came out with a mouth full of socks.

Adam Joshua gave George an old broken space spy, and an old ball with some bounce still in it, and he took the good socks out of George's mouth and gave him two that didn't match instead.

"These things can be yours," Adam Joshua told George. "So you can feel at home here. With these things," he said, "you'll like it fine."

Adam Joshua put George back in his corner and turned out the light.

It didn't work.

George fell over things in the dark, and ran into things in the dark, and Adam Joshua could hear things crashing down. George made it to the side of Adam Joshua's bed, and stood there bouncing on his short legs until one leg made it to the top. He used it to pull the rest of him up too.

"It figures," said Adam Joshua, getting up to get Fred.

George wiggled in Adam Joshua's bed, and rolled, and nipped, and nibbled. Out his window, Adam Joshua could see Nelson with his light still on, lying on his bed talking calmly to his fish.

"Go to sleep," Adam Joshua said, not calm, holding George down with both hands. "Now," he said, using his arms too. "Please!" he hollered.

———

When Adam Joshua woke up, George was sound asleep across his stomach. They were both holding onto Fred.

"Today," Adam Joshua said, waking up George, "you're going to learn tricks and how to save lives. By tonight," he told George, "you'll be so brave you won't even know it's you."

Adam Joshua gave George breakfast. Then

43

he ate his breakfast, and then he kept Amanda Jane from making a breakfast out of George's ears.

"You've got to quit that!" he shouted at Amanda Jane, pulling ears out of her mouth and putting in a piece of banana instead. "You can't go around eating other people's dogs," he told her, handing her a piece of apple too.

He took George out to meet Nelson.

"You'll like Nelson in no time," Adam Joshua told George, drying his ears for him on the way. "But you might not think so at first," he said.

Nelson backed away the minute he saw George.

"Why, Adam Joshua, that's a dog!" he said. "I don't like dogs."

"You'll like my dog, Nelson," said Adam Joshua. "His name is George and he's going to learn tricks and save my life one day. He's my good friend, Nelson," said Adam Joshua, putting George down.

George galloped over to bark at Nelson's shoelaces and say, "Hi!" Nelson backed up

until he was against the tree house ladder, and then he used the ladder to climb halfway up the tree.

"You should have told me you wanted a pet," Nelson said from the tree house. "I would have helped you pick a fish. I'm terrific at it," he said.

"Nelson," said Adam Joshua, "I wanted a dog. I like dogs, Nelson," said Adam Joshua. "I love dogs, Nelson. I hate fish!" he said, picking up George and taking him out in the yard to teach him things.

"Adam Joshua," Nelson yelled after him, "I probably would even have given you a fish!"

———

Adam Joshua tried to teach George things. Nelson watched from the tree house.

He tried to teach George to come when he called, "Here, George!"

He tried to teach George to sit when he said, "Sit, George!"

Adam Joshua tried to teach George to bring back a stick when he threw it, or when he said,

"Fetch!" or when he said, "Get it!" or when
he yelled, "Stick!"

George came when he shouldn't and didn't
when he should. George fell in a bush, and
tripped over his ears, and tumbled into the
tree getting to the stick, and when he got there
he lay down and chewed it up.

"George," sighed Adam Joshua, throwing

a new stick, "if you won't learn things how do you ever expect to save my life?"

Adam Joshua lay on the ground and pretended to be near a rattlesnake while George watched. He lay on the ground and pretended to be drowning while George watched. Adam Joshua lay on the ground and pretended to be in an avalanche, and in a hurricane, and trapped with an earthquake all around him while George watched.

"Come on, George, save my life!" he yelled. George lay on the ground watching Adam Joshua and fell asleep.

"George," sighed Adam Joshua, "you don't have an ounce of Kansas dog in you."

———

"Look at this book," said Nelson, coming down from the tree house. "Look at this book," he said. "It tells all about fish. You're going to love it!"

"Nelson," yelled Adam Joshua, "I don't want to know anything about fish. I have a dog, Nelson. Nelson," he shouted, "I love my dog!"

"Just read the book, Adam Joshua," Nelson

said, leaving it on the ground by the tree. "Everybody makes mistakes. It's never too late for a fish."

———

George went up to Adam Joshua's room. Adam Joshua followed soon after. When he got there he couldn't believe what he saw. The chewed-up head of one of Adam Joshua's space spies was in "GEORGE'S CORNER," the chewed-up body was by the bed, one chewed-up leg was by the dresser, and the other was in George's mouth being chewed up right then.

"Drop it!" yelled Adam Joshua.

George dropped it and bounced over to Adam Joshua.

"No bouncing!" yelled Adam Joshua, grabbing the space spy's head and body and legs, and trying to fit them all back together again.

Adam Joshua yelled, and George stopped bouncing.

Adam Joshua yelled, and George crawled under Adam Joshua's bed until only his tail stuck out.

Adam Joshua crawled under there with him.

"George," he said, nose to nose with George under the bed. "I'm sorry I yelled. But you don't go around chewing up people's people. You just don't."

George licked Adam Joshua's nose.

"Okay, as long as you're sorry," said Adam Joshua.

He sighed while he cleaned up. He used to have a baby who lived in his room and chewed up his space spies, and tore up his posters, and shredded other things that got in her way. Now he had George, who did all those things and slept on his stomach besides.

———

While they were getting ready for bed, Adam Joshua held George up to see the picture from Great-Aunt Emily.

"This dog was just like you," Adam Joshua told George. "This dog learned all the tricks that Great-Aunt Emily wanted to teach him. This dog saved her life one day."

George looked at the picture, then bit the frame and licked the glass. He turned to Adam Joshua's ear and bit and licked at it too.

"That's what I thought you'd say," said Adam Joshua. He got into bed, and let George lie across his stomach and settle down. Fred covered them both.

Nelson's shade was up, and his light was on. Then Adam Joshua saw Nelson's shade go down, and he sort-of-saw a hand writing across it in the dark.

The hand went away. Adam Joshua waited. The hand came back with a flashlight.

"**A FISH**," Adam Joshua read as the hand moved the flashlight across the shade, "**WILL NEVER LET YOU DOWN**."

After Nelson's shade had gone back up,

Adam Joshua lay very still while George went to sleep, and watched Nelson talking to his fish.

Nelson looked serious while he explained things to his fish, but sometimes he would smile, and once in a while he'd laugh.

It was too far for Adam Joshua to see the faces of Nelson's fish, but he thought they were probably paying close attention and agreeing with everything Nelson said.

Adam Joshua had never tried to talk to George like that.

"George?" said Adam Joshua.

George stirred in his sleep. His ears went down further over his eyes.

Adam Joshua went right ahead and told him things anyway.

———

In the morning, Adam Joshua took George to meet Nelson again.

"I like my friends to like my friends," said Adam Joshua, trying to hand George to Nelson.

"I'm allergic to dogs," Nelson said, backing

away and climbing the tree house ladder up to the tree house.

"That's just fine," Adam Joshua yelled after Nelson. He patted George and gave him a hug, so that George wouldn't feel bad. "My dog's allergic to Nelsons too!" he shouted.

For a while, Adam Joshua worked hard at teaching George tricks.

For a while, George worked hard at not learning them.

"Good dog," said Adam Joshua, patting George on the head anyway. "Why, you're catching on fine."

"Adam Joshua," Nelson called from the tree house. "You should never lie to a dog."

Adam Joshua carried George into the house to try teaching him things where Nelson couldn't watch. Amanda Jane went crawling by.

"She didn't work out too well at first, either," Adam Joshua said. He shoved the furniture in the living room back, so there would be more room for throwing sticks. "But she's getting better," he told George.

That night, while George slept on his stomach, Adam Joshua thought about George.

George, he thought, wasn't exactly the dog he had had in mind. But now that he had him, he couldn't think of any other dog being George.

Adam Joshua wasn't sure George was turning out that great as a dog, but he thought he was turning out fine as a friend.

Sometimes lately, when Adam Joshua told Nelson about things that bothered him, or things that he worried about, or things that scared him at night, Nelson laughed.

George didn't do that.

Sometimes lately, when Adam Joshua told Nelson about the special things he thought about, or the things he dreamed of doing someday, if Nelson didn't understand them, he'd laugh.

But Adam Joshua had started telling George all his worries, and bothers, and scares, and thoughts, and dreams, and George hadn't laughed once.

Of course, Adam Joshua had to wait until

George was asleep so he'd hold still long enough to tell him anything.

But still, Adam Joshua thought, George never laughed.

———

In the morning, Adam Joshua carried George up some of the steps to the tree house, and he pushed George up some, and helped him climb the rest.

"Adam Joshua," yelled Nelson when they got to the top. "What do you think you're doing? Dogs don't belong in tree houses. No dog belongs in my tree house!"

Adam Joshua lay down to pant a bit, and George lay beside him to pant along.

"Nelson," said Adam Joshua, lying there. "It's my tree house too, and it's my dog, and my dog wanted to see what my tree house was like. Nelson," he said, pointing, "you always bring your fish here and I never complain."

"Fish," said Nelson, moving himself and the fishbowl as far away from George as he could, "are nothing to complain about, Adam Joshua."

———

Nelson sat on his side of the tree house and read, with his fishbowl by his side.

Adam Joshua lay on his side of the tree house and thought about things. George stayed beside him, thinking too.

Nobody said anything.

Suddenly, George stopped thinking and sat up. George saw the fishbowl and started howling. He jumped over Adam Joshua, and jumped over Nelson, and put his nose into the fishbowl.

Nelson started howling.

"Adam Joshua! Your dog is trying to eat my fish. That dog is dangerous!" he howled. "Out of my tree house! And take your killer dog with you!"

Adam Joshua and George went down the tree house steps faster than they'd gone up them.

"Adam Joshua," Nelson shouted after him, "I don't know how long I can put up with a best friend who has a dog like that. That's asking a lot from anybody!"

Adam Joshua took George up to his bedroom, telling him things all the way.

"Don't you worry about it," he told George. "That kid doesn't know anything. You'll be a real Kansas dog and save my life someday," said Adam Joshua. "You don't have an ounce of killer in you."

Outside, Nelson sat in the tree house, reading to his fish.

"That's not fair," said Adam Joshua, watching through his window. He got his marker.

He crawled under his window, shot his hand up fast, and pulled his shade down low.

"**TREE HOUSE SCHEDUJE**," Adam Joshua wrote.

"**ADAM JOSHUA AND GEORGE**," he wrote. "**NEJSON WITH FISH**." Adam Joshua counted up days and the hours in them, and he took half and gave Nelson the rest.

"**AND IT'S OUR TURN NOW!**" he wrote.

———

"You've put on weight since the last time," Adam Joshua told George, pulling him up the tree house steps, and pushing him up, and shoving him too.

Before he'd gone, Nelson had used chalk to draw the line back down the middle of the tree house.

"**FISH**," he wrote on his side. "**DOGS**," he wrote on the other.

"**DOGS WHO TRESPASS WILL BE EATEN**," he had written on his floor, and he drew a big mean fish with big mean teeth, smiling.

"Of course there's always the chance you'll never get used to Nelson," Adam Joshua told George. He burst out laughing and hugged George tight.

The Superman Kid

"The new Superman movie is coming!" the man on TV told Adam Joshua. "You've got to see it!"

"The new Superman movie is coming!" Adam Joshua yelled, zooming out to the tree house to tell Nelson. "We've got to see it!"

"Well, that will be nice, Adam Joshua," said

61

Nelson, as he swept his side of the tree house. "I like movies."

"Nice?" said Adam Joshua. "Like? Nelson, it's not just a movie. It's the real life story of Superman. We love Superman, Nelson. He's our hero. We've been waiting for this movie for a long time."

"You've been waiting, maybe. But I think I've outgrown superheroes," Nelson said. "I just don't believe in Superman anymore. He's a legend."

Adam Joshua could hardly believe Nelson had said that.

"You believe in other people who are legends, Nelson," he said. "You believe in Santa Claus."

Nelson stopped sweeping for a minute to think about it.

"Santa Claus brings me presents and candy," he said, getting back to work. "That makes a difference, you know, Adam Joshua."

———

Adam Joshua practiced each day to get ready for Superman. He practiced speeding faster than a bullet, and he practiced being more powerful than a locomotive, and he practiced bending bars of steel in his bare hands.

"Put that fork down," his mother said, catching him at it. "That's the third one this week."

"I'm just visiting," Adam Joshua told her. "From a distant planet. If I were you," he said, "I'd be nicer about forks."

His mother looked him straight in the eye

and bent the fork back to its shape in her bare hands.

"Then again," Adam Joshua said, watching her, "it's entirely up to you how you treat your guests."

————

"Almost," the man on TV told Adam Joshua.

"Almost," Adam Joshua called out his bedroom window to Nelson.

"Fine, Adam Joshua," Nelson called back.

Adam Joshua practiced looking through doors with his X-ray vision. He practiced his leaping and bounding and flying.

He practiced fast changes.

"Out," said his mother. "Out of the pantry, and out of the kitchen, and out into the backyard while you're at it."

"But it's all I've got," said Adam Joshua, coming out of the kitchen pantry with one pant leg on, and one shoe on, and no shirt on, and the Superman cape his mother made him twisted around his neck.

"I don't have a phone booth," he told her.

But this is near the phone, so I use it. It's all I've got," he said.

"No, you don't," said his mother, shoving him right out the back door, and tossing his clothes after him.

"Don't forget I'm just visiting," Adam Joshua shouted as the back door slammed. "From another planet!" he yelled.

"And she's going to feel really terrible when she finds out she's treated a guest that way," he muttered to his shoe as he finished getting dressed.

———

"Out!" shouted Nelson. "Out of the tree house, Adam Joshua! All of your jumping around and shouting at things is driving me crazy and scaring my fish."

"But Nelson," said Adam Joshua, rescuing Clyde/Irving from his box and whizzing him right by Nelson's head. "You're my best friend, Nelson," said Adam Joshua. "You should understand."

"I don't understand anything," said Nelson, rescuing Clyde/Irving from Adam Joshua and putting him back in his box. "I don't under-stand you," said Nelson, untying the Super-man cape from under Adam Joshua's chin. "Grown kids don't fly around wearing capes, Adam Joshua!" yelled Nelson, flinging the cape down the tree house stairs. "Out!" he shouted.

Adam Joshua knocked on Clyde/Irving's shell before he went.

"I'm here if you need me," said Adam Joshua. "Just whistle and I'll come."

———

"You only need to wait a little longer," said the man on TV.

"Great Galaxies!" said Adam Joshua.

"I may look meek and mild-mannered to you," he told Amanda Jane, flying by on his way to supper and stopping to give her a kiss, "but underneath it all," he said, "I'm a kid of iron."

"Kryptonite!" he shouted when he saw the bowl of broccoli on the table.

"Take it away, take it away!" he yelled, throwing up an arm to shield himself from the sight, and falling off his chair, and rolling around on the floor getting ready to die.

"It'll do me in," he whispered.

Amanda Jane leaned out of her high chair to see what was doing him in and dropped a carrot in his ear.

"If the kryptonite doesn't do you in, I'm going to," his mother said, putting extra broccoli on his plate.

———

Nelson was playing in his yard after supper with Henry. Nelson put his arms around Henry to protect him the minute Adam Joshua showed up.

"Don't you dare try to fly with this baby," said Nelson.

"Nelson," said Adam Joshua, "if it wasn't for Superman the world would be terrible.

"Superman," said Adam Joshua, "saves people, and stops trains when they're running away, and holds up bridges when they're cracking.

"Superman," said Adam Joshua, "catches bad guys, and helps good guys, and never tells a lie."

"Superman," said Nelson, picking up Henry to go inside, "is made up and I've outgrown him."

"Superman really likes kids," said Adam Joshua. "And he'd be really mad if he knew you felt that way!"

―――――

"It's here! It's here!" the man on TV shouted at Adam Joshua.

"And about time!" Adam Joshua shouted right along.

He flew down the hall, and through the

living room, and into the kitchen, and he picked up Amanda Jane on his way by.

"Baby's getting heavy," he panted, sort-of-flying into the living room again, and putting Amanda Jane down with a *splot* on the floor, and sitting himself down with one too.

"Put that baby down," his mother said, after he already had. "You can't do that!" she said.

"Used to be able to," Adam Joshua said, panting hard.

———

Adam Joshua found his Superman undershorts in a corner of the closet. He found his Superman undershirt stuffed down in the bottom of his hamper.

"Still look fine," he said, pounding the wrinkles out of them with his fist.

He looked through his shirts until he found an old one with only one button left. He could unbutton it in a hurry in case he was needed.

Adam Joshua pulled his Superman cape out of his closet, and his Superman blue pants out from under his bed, and his Superman glasses out from a drawer where he kept things like that.

"I can't believe it," said Adam Joshua, looking at a new hole George had chewed in his cape.

He put on his one-button shirt, and the cape with the hole in it, and he put on his blue pants, and he put on his glasses.

George walked by the door, and backed up to come in, and looked at Adam Joshua dressed like Superman, and growled.

Adam Joshua got down, nose to nose with George, and growled back.

"Listen," Adam Joshua told George, scratching him on the stomach, "if you aren't going to learn to save lives, somebody's got to do it."

———

"Fifteen minutes," his father called. "The baby-sitter for Amanda Jane's already here."

"Just finishing up," Adam Joshua called back. He found his Superman ring and his Superman medal and put them on. He dug for his

71

Superman cologne, and he splashed some behind his ears. He slipped on his red galoshes.

Then he looked in the mirror.

Superman looked right back at him.

"Don't you worry," Adam Joshua said. "Your
identity's safe with me."

"I can't believe it," said Nelson, standing in
the doorway, looking at Adam Joshua dressed
up in the cape, and the galoshes, and the sunglasses.

"I can't believe it, either," said Adam Joshua,
looking at Nelson dressed in his best shirt, and
his best shoes, and his tie.

"I like ties," said Nelson.

———

When they got to the movie theater there
was a big line waiting.

"Waiting again," Adam Joshua sighed, as
they took their place at the end of the line.

In the line there were kids talking about
Superman, and acting like Superman, and in
the line there were some kids who dressed up
to look like him too.

"I just don't believe it," Nelson kept saying, and he kept right on straightening his tie each time he said it.

Adam Joshua turned around and looked eye-to-eye into the eyes of other sunglasses just like his.

Adam Joshua didn't blink. The other kid didn't blink.

Adam Joshua reached down slowly to the one button on his shirt, and unbuttoned it.

"Pow!" he yelled, pulling open his shirt to show his true identity.

The other kid didn't say anything. He reached down and unbuttoned three buttons on his shirt and showed Adam Joshua an undershirt just like his.

"Pow!" he whispered.

"Let's get this line moving," Adam Joshua said, turning around and buttoning his shirt again. "There are some strange characters here," he told his father.

———

Adam Joshua picked the row of seats, and then he picked his seat.

"Perfect," he said.

A tall man with a lot of hair came and sat right down in front of him.

Adam Joshua changed seats with his mother, and he changed seats with his father, and he made Nelson change seats with him.

"Now, that's fine," he said, as he got everyone settled down again. "Now, everyone sit quiet," said Adam Joshua as the lights went down and the screen lit up with Superman flying fast across it.

Adam Joshua jumped out of his seat to fly right along.

"Shh," said his mother. "Shh," said three people behind him.

"Adam Joshua," said Nelson. "Sit down!"

———

Superman flew high and flew low and caught everybody bad in between.

Superman waged a ceaseless battle against crime. Adam Joshua waged it right up there with him.

Superman fought hard for truth, and he fought hard for justice, and he fought super hard for The American Way. Adam Joshua was by his side.

Superman kissed his favorite girl.

"That's terrible," said Adam Joshua, scrunching down in his seat with his hands over his eyes.

"You can't trust anybody, Adam Joshua," said Nelson, scrunching down in the seat beside him with his eyes covered too.

———

"The biggest drink," Adam Joshua whispered to his father about refreshments. "The one that comes in the Superman glass you get to keep."

"You can't drink all that," his father whispered back. "That's more than you can handle."

"The biggest," Adam Joshua said, forgetting to whisper. "In the glass."

"Shh," the three people in back and his mother all said.

"I'll just take the little drink," whispered Nelson. "I don't need a glass to keep."

Adam Joshua's drink came in a white shiny

glass. Adam Joshua had to hold it with two
hands, and he used his knee to hold it up from
underneath.

While the villains were looking for Superman, Adam Joshua drank. While Superman
was looking for the villains, Adam Joshua
drank. While everybody talked about everybody looking for everybody, Adam Joshua
drank.

By the time everybody was through talking
and Superman and the villains had found each
other and were getting ready to fight, Adam

Joshua was through drinking and had to go to the bathroom.

"Shh," said his mother as he got up and made his way across a lot of people's knees to get to the aisle. "Shh, shh, shh," said the three people behind.

By the time Adam Joshua got back the fight was finished.

"You missed the best part," whispered Nelson.

———

"Not bad," Nelson said calmly, straightening his tie and yawning as they walked out of the theater. Adam Joshua glared at Nelson and flashed his shirt open wide.

All the way home, Nelson talked with Adam Joshua's parents about the movie.

"Nice special effects," Nelson told Adam Joshua's father.

"Good photography too," he said.

All the way home, Adam Joshua thought about looking like Superman and flying like Superman, and fighting evil the way Superman fights it.

"Pow!" Adam Joshua whispered to himself.

"I especially enjoyed the plot," said Nelson.

At home, Adam Joshua rescued George, who was sleeping.

George, who was sleeping, woke up and barked, and saw it was Adam Joshua rescuing him, and licked his nose.

"No thanks needed," said Adam Joshua.

Adam Joshua rescued Amanda Jane, who was sleeping.

"Cut that out!" said his mother, putting Amanda Jane back to bed.

Adam Joshua rescued his mother right where she stood, patting Amanda Jane to sleep again.

"My hero," his mother said, bending down to kiss him.

"Last time *she* gets saved," Adam Joshua said, flying out of the room, spitting a lot.

Out his window, Adam Joshua could see Nelson untying his tie in the mirror and talking to his fish.

Adam Joshua flew around his room four times with his cape spread wide behind him.

"Adam Joshua, Superkid!" he said, screeching to a stop in front of his mirror.

Looking back at him was Adam Joshua in a cape that had a hole chewed there by George. Looking back at him was Adam Joshua in a shirt with one button, and a wrinkled undershirt, and red galoshes, and blue pants that had grown too little.

"We were great!" said both Adam Joshuas.

———

He took off his cape. He took off his shirt with one button, and his blue pants, and his underwear, and his galoshes. He sort of folded everything and stuffed it all away in his bottom dresser drawer. He put on his pajamas with Superman flying fast across the top.

Adam Joshua turned out the light and crawled into bed with George.

"Don't you worry," he told George. "I remember every minute and everything that Superman did in the movie, and I'll tell you all about it."

George yawned and closed his eyes.

"But you mustn't get too excited about it,"

said Adam Joshua, "or you'll never get to sleep."

Adam Joshua told George all about the flying and the fighting.

He didn't tell him a thing about the kissing.

Out his window, Adam Joshua could see Nelson telling his fish about the photography and the plot.

"I'm really worried about that kid," Adam Joshua told George.

Adam Joshua saw Nelson go into his closet and pull the door shut.

Adam Joshua waited but Nelson didn't come out.

"Excuse me," Adam Joshua said, scooting out from underneath George. "I'll finish telling you things in a minute."

Adam Joshua stood at his window and used his binoculars to study Nelson's room. Everything in Nelson's room looked very neat. His tie was on the dresser. His fish were asleep in their bowl. Nelson was in his closet.

Adam Joshua waited. Nelson didn't come out.

Adam Joshua studied the bottom of the closet

door with his binoculars to see if Nelson was trying to send smoke signals or messages out underneath it. But there was no sign from Nelson.

All of a sudden Nelson's closet door flew open and Nelson flew out of it, and he flew around his room twice with his arms out and his cape spread wide behind him.

The closet door banged back all the way, and on the inside of it Adam Joshua could see a big poster of Superman.

"Great Galaxies!" said Adam Joshua.

Nelson had on his red rubber boots, and blue pants, and a red and blue striped shirt. He had on a cape that Adam Joshua had never seen before, but it must have been a cape that Nelson had in his closet all along.

"You'll never believe it either," Adam Joshua said, waking up George and carrying him to the window.

Nelson zoomed around his room, and he flew high and flew low, and he picked up his fish to try flying with them.

Adam Joshua and George watched as Nel-

son stopped to put his fish back on their table and mopped up fish water with his cape. Then Nelson climbed up on his bed to get a leaping start. He looked out the window.

Adam Joshua ducked so Nelson wouldn't see him, and he made George duck too.

When he came up again, Nelson's shade was down.

"I know just how you feel," Adam Joshua said as he took George over and dumped him in bed. He went to his bottom dresser drawer and got out his cape.

"But I don't want to hear a word about it," he said, crawling in bed with George and using the cape to cover them both.

A Visit From Cynthia

Nelson's cousin, Cynthia, was coming to stay for a bit.

"And it's going to be awful, Adam Joshua," said Nelson. "I haven't seen her since I was a baby, but I know she's a girl. And what are we going to do with a girl?"

There were some kinds of girls Adam Joshua liked, but there were other kinds he couldn't stand. "What kind of a girl, Nelson?" Adam Joshua asked.

"Well, my mother says sweet," said Nelson, "but I think she means gooey. And my mother says she's quiet and good," said Nelson, "but

I'll bet that means she won't want to do any of the things we like to do. I think we're in a lot of trouble, Adam Joshua."

Adam Joshua nodded along with Nelson. That was exactly the kind of girl he hated. He sat for a minute, thinking about it.

"You know, Superman seems to like all kinds of girls," he finally said. "And you know, Nelson, I've always worried about that."

———

When Cynthia got there, she was very quiet.

"Just a little shy," said Nelson's mother, straightening a bow on one of Cynthia's braids and giving her a pat on the shoulder to help her feel brave.

"You boys be gentle with her," whispered Nelson's mother. "She's older than you but she's nervous and shy and needs time to adjust. Very gentle," said Nelson's mother, straightening the other one of Cynthia's bows and going inside.

Adam Joshua and Nelson stood staring at Cynthia, and Cynthia stood staring at the ground.

Cynthia didn't say anything.

Nelson didn't say anything.

"Nice bows," said Adam Joshua.

Cynthia stopped staring at the ground and raised her eyes and stood staring at Adam Joshua and Nelson. She put a hand on a bow and smiled.

It was a horrible smile. It was a smile full of big yellow teeth, and full of broken braces that glittered in the sun, and it had a lot of meanness mixed right in.

Cynthia smiled and yanked at her bows, and her hair came out of its braids and shot out in spikes all over her head.

"Move it!" said Cynthia, throwing the bows over her shoulders.

"Follow me!" she said, marching for the tree house. "We've got a lot to get done, and I've only got a few days to get things organized."

Cynthia pulled a pair of sunglasses out of her pocket and put them on. They were the kind of sunglasses that hid eyes, and had mirrors where the lenses should be.

Adam Joshua hated sunglasses like that.

"I thought your mother said she'd be sweet and quiet," Adam Joshua whispered, following along scared.

"My mother's been wrong before," whispered Nelson, scared and right behind him.

In the tree house Cynthia got things organized. She put Nelson and Adam Joshua in a corner and made them stay there.

"You little kids don't get in my way," she told them. "Don't even think it!

"This junk's got to go," said Cynthia, picking up their pinecone collections, and their rock collections, and their marble collections, and their seashells, and dumping them all over the side.

"Kid stuff," said Cynthia, ripping down the Superman poster, and sending it over the side too.

"Now, hold on a minute!" shouted Adam Joshua. He stood up and faced Cynthia at about her neck.

Cynthia looked Adam Joshua over closely.

"At home I've got big snakes," she said. "They eat rats whole. And you're not much bigger than a rat," she said, picking Adam Joshua up and putting him back in the corner again.

"The turtle," said Cynthia, slipping Clyde/Irving in her pocket, "is mine."

———

Cynthia put up posters of the kind of monsters that Adam Joshua and Nelson didn't even like to think about. Next she put out her collections.

"Snakeskins," she said, putting out boxes. "Spiders," she said, putting out jars. "And bones, Adam Joshua," she said, waving one under his nose. "I don't have any people bones," Cynthia said, separating the big bones from the small. "Not yet. But I'm working on it."

Cynthia finished getting organized by writing big across the tree house wall.

"CYNTHIA'S PLACE!!!" she wrote.

It looked just like Cynthia's place. There was nothing of Adam Joshua or Nelson left there at all.

———

That night Adam Joshua sat around trying to think what to do about Cynthia.

"I can't think of a thing," he told George.

Later that night, Nelson showed up at Adam Joshua's door with his fishbowl held tight in his arms.

"Adam Joshua," whispered Nelson, "hide my fish. You never can tell what she's going to try to organize next."

In the morning when Adam Joshua looked out his window, Cynthia was already in the tree house with Nelson tucked in the corner. Cynthia was talking to her spiders. Nelson wasn't saying a word.

"Keep the dog and the baby inside," Adam Joshua told his mother on his way through the kitchen. "Outside they wouldn't stand a chance."

———

"You don't have to keep coming back," Nelson whispered to Adam Joshua when he climbed into the tree house. "She's not your cousin, and she's not your problem, and you don't have to come."

"I'll come," whispered Adam Joshua. "You're my friend and you need me. Without me," whispered Adam Joshua, looking at Cynthia with her braces glittering in the sun, "she'd have you eaten in no time."

"Sit down and get quiet," said Cynthia.

Adam Joshua and Nelson sat down. They got quiet.

"It's my tree house now, and we go by my rules now, and now you do what I say," said Cynthia, standing there with her hands on her hips, looking down at Adam Joshua and Nelson.

"Any questions?" asked Cynthia.

Nobody had any questions.

In Cynthia's sunglasses Adam Joshua could see himself and Nelson sitting quiet and little and hardly there at all. While Cynthia talked the sun made her braces flash like barbed wire. When Cynthia stopped talking and smiled, it was even worse.

"Superman," Adam Joshua whispered to Nelson, "would know what to do about this.

"Superman," Adam Joshua whispered to Nelson, "would take care of her in no time."

"Terrific, Adam Joshua," Nelson whispered back, trying to get more comfortable in the corner. "Then get him fast," he said.

"Today we play games," said Cynthia. "I love games."

Cynthia knew games that made Adam Joshua and Nelson shiver in their shoes.

"In this game," Cynthia said, "I pretend to roast you alive and eat you whole.

"In the next game," Cynthia said, "I pretend to skin you first."

Adam Joshua and Nelson played Cynthia's

games, and they played by her rules, and they did what she told them to do.

They hated it.

They kept playing games, and then Cynthia got hungry and made Adam Joshua and Nelson get her food. They hated that too, but they did it.

Cynthia ate and then she got sleepy. She made Adam Joshua and Nelson polish the bones in her collection while she took a nap in the tree house.

"And I only sleep with one eye," said Cynthia. "The other one will be wide awake watching you."

———

"I should do something, Adam Joshua," said Nelson, polishing hard on a bone. "She's my cousin and it's up to me. It's just," he said, "that I don't know what to do. I'm not very brave, Adam Joshua," said Nelson.

Adam Joshua felt the same way about Nelson, but he didn't think he should let Nelson know it.

"You've helped me with a lot of my problems, Nelson," he said, polishing hard too. "Why, you've been brave about all my problems."

"Problems that belong to other people are easy, Adam Joshua," said Nelson. "Cousins that belong to you," he said, picking up a new bone and sighing, "really aren't the same thing at all."

99

That night, Adam Joshua lay on his bed and worried some more about Nelson. George lay beside him worrying too.

"Somebody needs to take care of him," Adam Joshua told George.

George growled.

"Right," said Adam Joshua, rubbing George's nose. "I know how you feel about saving lives," he said, "but you can't do everything all by yourself."

Adam Joshua saw Nelson's shade go down and Nelson's hand go up behind it.

"**ADAM JOSHUA**," the hand wrote, "**I HAVE A GREAT IDEA ABOUT**—"

Another hand, one wearing a spider ring, came up under the shade and grabbed the hand belonging to Nelson. The hand took away the marker and rolled the shade up with a snap.

Adam Joshua put on his Superman cape and flew around the room with George right behind.

"Zam, zap, Cynthia!" he shouted. "Zow, zing!

"POW!" he yelled out his window over at Nelson's window and Cynthia. Then he pulled his shade down fast just in case Cynthia was looking out and could see him.

———

"What do you do about a bully?" Adam Joshua asked his mother the next morning at breakfast. "A big one. And mean."

"Most bullies are really cowards," said his mother. "Most bullies are afraid of things, and they don't feel very good about themselves, so they act like bullies. Usually a bully will back off if you stand up to him."

"Her," said Adam Joshua.

"Her," said his mother.

"What if your bully isn't usual?" asked Adam Joshua. "What if you stand up to her and she gets mad?"

"Then you get hurt," said his mother.

"That's pretty much what I thought," said Adam Joshua, pushing the rest of his breakfast away.

———

"You look terrible, Nelson," Adam Joshua whispered to Nelson in the tree house corner. "Why, Nelson, you look really bad."

"Cynthia," said Nelson, "isn't an easy person to live with, Adam Joshua. She plays tricks. The first night she put her biggest hairy spider in my bed, and it crawled right up my pajama leg before I knew it was there. Last night it was a bone under my pillow, and later she threw a snakeskin on me. A person," said Nelson, "doesn't sleep well after all that."

"What about your great idea, Nelson?" Adam Joshua asked. "The one you wrote on your shade. What about that?"

"Never mind, Adam Joshua," whispered Nelson, yawning. "It wasn't that great. It wasn't even good."

———

"Today," said Cynthia, "I have a whole list of new games. I'm just going to love today," she said, and she smiled.

Adam Joshua and Nelson played the new games. They were the worst games they had ever played in their lives. They polished Cynthia's bones, and helped her look in the yard and in the garbage for new ones.

They brought her food.

"Red meat," said Cynthia. "Hard bread. Lemonade."

"She's good around my mother, Adam Joshua," said Nelson, polishing bones while Cynthia slept with one eye. "Around my mother she's fine.

"And even when I tell my mother, Adam Joshua," said Nelson, "even when I tell my mother all about her, my mother doesn't believe it all. My mother says nobody that good can be that bad.

"Then," said Nelson, rubbing his polishing arm for a minute, "my mother says even if she was that bad, we'd still have to put up with most of it. My mother says when you have guests sometimes you have to put up with a lot. Cynthia's more than a lot to put up with, Adam Joshua," said Nelson. "She's a whole lot more."

"We could always say no, Nelson," whispered Adam Joshua, polishing his bone harder as Cynthia woke up and started stretching. "I'll bet we could just say no," Adam Joshua whispered again, trying to make his whisper sound brave.

"Once," said Cynthia, standing up to finish her stretch, "there was a kid I told to do something and he told me he didn't want to do it. He said, 'No.'"

Adam Joshua got up fast to go get Cynthia some more lemonade.

"He's still looking for his teeth," Cynthia yelled after him.

———

"What do you do when you think you should be brave, but you don't know how to be?" Adam Joshua asked his father. "What do you do if you're afraid to be brave?"

"Everyone's afraid to be brave," Adam Joshua's father told him. "Otherwise they wouldn't need to be brave to do what they do.

"But you have to be wise about being brave," said Adam Joshua's father, scratching George

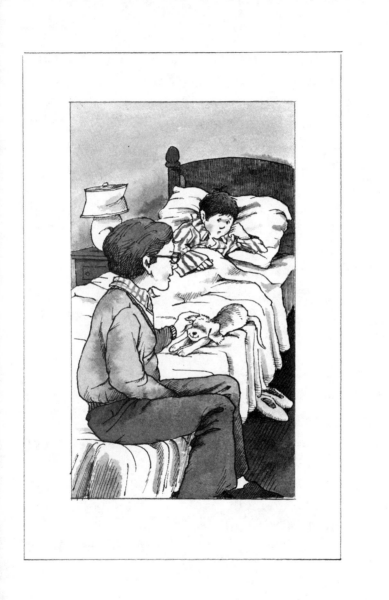

behind the ears until he was almost asleep. "You have to decide if it's worth it. Because it's one thing to be brave," said his father, covering Adam Joshua and George up with the cover after covering them with Fred first, "and it's another to be foolish."

———

"I know how you feel," Adam Joshua told George the next morning, when George stood at the door, whining to go out to play.

"I know you want to be with me, and I know you're brave," he told George. "But you need to get smart too," he said, giving George a kiss on the nose and leaving him there.

———

"We could hit her, Adam Joshua," said Nelson, while they looked for flies to feed Cynthia's spiders. "You could hit her."

"I'm just not a hitting kind of person," said Adam Joshua. "I didn't even hit when I was a baby. Amanda Jane doesn't even hit." Adam Joshua thought about it. "She bites a bit, though," he said.

"Maybe we could pounce on her, Adam

106

Joshua," said Nelson, killing a fly and looking sad about it. "If you'd pounce first, I'd be right behind you."

"I'm not any good at pouncing either," Adam Joshua said. He got ready to kill a fly and then let it go because it looked like it had things to do.

"If we do anything about her," said Nelson, closing his eyes tight, and hitting a fly fast, "we're going to get hurt. It seems to me that it's better to do what she wants and wait till she leaves. I don't know how long she'll be here, Adam Joshua," said Nelson. "The hurting could go on for days."

Adam Joshua and Nelson fed flies to spiders, and they fed food to Cynthia, and they settled down to the bones.

"Okay, Nelson," whispered Adam Joshua. "We've put up with a lot so far. We can keep putting up with it. But Nelson," said Adam Joshua, "everybody's got a limit. We've got to have a limit too. We'll put up with things, but we'll have a limit about how much we'll put up with."

"I still wish I was braver," Nelson whispered.

They watched Cynthia pick up a jar of spiders to talk to them. A big fat hairy one looked like it was talking back.

"Sometimes, Nelson," said Adam Joshua, "you can confuse being brave with being foolish."

Cynthia wrapped a snakeskin around her neck and stroked it.

"Or really dumb," he said.

———

"So don't worry," Adam Joshua told George, scratching him behind the ears to help him get to sleep that night. "We've got our limit, and we can put up with things until then. But I know if we need you," Adam Joshua told George, "you'll be right there."

The first thing Adam Joshua saw when he woke up in the morning was a stick sticking out of Nelson's window. At the end of the stick was a sock, and a note was pinned to it.

"**WAR!!!**" yelled the note.

Adam Joshua jumped up and got dressed for war.

He got out his Superman underwear, and his blue pants, and his shirt with one button, and he dug his cape and galoshes out of the closet.

"I need you," he told George.

"Out of our way, Amanda Jane," Adam Joshua said, going past his sister in the kitchen, and picking her up to give her a kiss, and putting her out of the way.

"War," he told her, "is no place for a kid."

———

"My fish, Adam Joshua," said Nelson, meeting him under the tree and looking terrible. "I gave you most of my fish," he said, "but I had two that were sick. I kept them home to take care of them, and I hid them away.

"Adam Joshua," said Nelson, looking worse, "she flushed my fish. She found them, and she said nobody could be expected to live with sick fish.

"Adam Joshua," yelled Nelson, "she flushed my fish!"

"Nelson," hollered Adam Joshua, "do you mean we're going to fight because of two fish? Nelson," he shouted, "you mean we're going to finally get murdered because of two fish? Nelson," said Adam Joshua, sitting on the ground, tired, "I thought she had done something to *you*."

111

"Adam Joshua," said Nelson, sitting down too, "my fish *are* me." Tears started to roll down his cheeks.

Adam Joshua couldn't stand it when Nelson cried.

"Well, then, don't you worry," he said, hugging Nelson hard and wiping away some of the tears with his cape. "A limit's a limit, and a friend's a friend, and war's war," he said, unbuttoning his shirt.

———

"Cynthia," Adam Joshua yelled when Cynthia got to the tree house. "You've pushed us, and you've shoved us, and you've bossed us around. Cynthia," yelled Adam Joshua, "you've thrown out our stuff, and you've taken our turtle, and you've made us play games and do things we hate."

"You've flushed my fish," yelled Nelson.

George growled.

"Cynthia," said Adam Joshua, "I'm not good at hitting, but you take one more step and I'm going to hit you."

112

"And I'm going to help him," said Nelson, standing tall beside Adam Joshua. "And I kick too, Cynthia," said Nelson, quietly. "Hard."

"And I'm going to knock out your teeth," said Cynthia.

———

In the tree house there were pinecone collections, and marble collections, and seashells, and rocks.

Spiders and bones and snakeskins were gone.

The Superman poster was back up, looking a little the worse for wear. Adam Joshua and Nelson looked the same way.

Adam Joshua had a rip in his cape, and a bruise on his shoulder, and a bash on his knuckles, and a black eye.

Nelson had rips in his pants, and a scratch on his cheek, and a foot that felt broken, and an eye like Adam Joshua's.

But they both kept all their teeth.

"And it was worth it, Adam Joshua," said Nelson, stretching out on the floor of the tree house and taking off his shoe to rub his foot.

"Well, it was worth it," said Adam Joshua, stretching out too. He got back up.

He took out a marker and drew an X through where it said, "**CYNTHIA'S PLACE!!!**"

"Not anymore," he said. "**THIS PLACE BELONGS TO ADAM JOSHUA AND NELSON**," he wrote. "**AND ALWAYS WILL !!**"

"Make that Nelson and Adam Joshua," said Nelson.

Adam Joshua knocked on Clyde/Irving's shell.

"You can come out now," he said, "she's gone.

"I'll take George inside, Nelson," said Adam Joshua, going over to where George was resting from fighting Cynthia. One ear had a bend in it, and his tail dragged low.

"Don't even bother getting up," he told George. "I'll carry you all the way.

"After I take George inside, Nelson," said Adam Joshua, "I'll bring your fish out. You can sit with your fish in the tree house, and you'll feel fine."

"No hurry, Adam Joshua," said Nelson. "I'll

be glad to see my fish, but I'm feeling fine already. In fact, Adam Joshua," Nelson called after him, "I feel the finest I've felt in all my life!"

Cynthia's sunglasses were lying at the bottom of the tree house ladder.

Adam Joshua picked them up and put them on George so the sun wouldn't get in his eyes.

"Pow!" he said.

Nelson at Night

If you needed a friend you could always understand, and a friend who would always understand you, and a friend as much like you as a friend could be, you wouldn't choose Nelson.

And if you needed a friend who would always keep you laughing, and never let you down, and who would always do what you thought a friend should do—you wouldn't even want Nelson.

But if you needed a friend who made you happy sometimes, and sometimes made you

117

mad, and kept you trying hard to be a friend yourself, Nelson worked out fine.

Adam Joshua had pretty well figured out that was the way things between friends would be. He didn't always like it, but he was getting used to it.

"You know, Nelson," he said, as they sat in the tree house one morning, "you should come and stay all night with me. You've never stayed all night with me before. That would be a lot of fun!"

"Well, that would be a lot of fun," Nelson said. "I'll have to check to see if I can, but I know I can." Nelson zoomed down the tree house ladder.

Adam Joshua zoomed right after him. He'd just remembered he had to go check with his mother too.

"He's coming!" Adam Joshua told his mother later. "He just called and he says he's coming and he'll be here in an hour."

"Great!" said Adam Joshua's mother. "We'll get ready."

She went to the door of Adam Joshua's room and looked around.

"I'll get ready by starting supper," she said. "You get ready by cleaning this room."

Adam Joshua went to the door of his room, and stood beside his mother and looked around too.

From where he was standing he could see piles. There was a pile of dirty clothes tucked under his bed, and there was a pile of clean clothes falling out of his drawer because he had forgotten to close it. There was a pile in front of him made up of one red tennis shoe, one flat blue football, a green plastic pickle whistle, five pieces of a Batman puzzle, a gold seashell, and a lens out of his sunglasses. There was all of the twine from a roll that he had unwound and hadn't been able to wind back up.

On the other side of the room there was a pile exactly like it.

"It'll do fine," Adam Joshua told his mother. He closed his door. "Nelson likes me the way

119

I am," he said. "He'll like my room that way too."

"Clean," said his mother as she opened the door again. "You've got an hour."

———

Adam Joshua looked at his room, and sighed, and got ready to clean it.

He looked through three piles until he found his clock, and he plugged it in. He picked out a time and set it.

"One hour," he said, looking around.

Adam Joshua started on clothes. He pulled most of the dirty clothes out from under the bed and piled them on top of the bed. He pulled dirty shirts and dirty jeans and dirty socks out from other piles and put them on top of the bed too. He tried to close the drawer with the clean clothes in it, but it was stuck. Adam Joshua took all the clean clothes out of the drawer, and put them with the dirty clothes on the bed, and carried them all down and put them in the hamper in the laundry room.

"One job done," he said, starting on a new pile.

Adam Joshua found one marble in the new pile, and three marbles in another pile, and a bunch in "GEORGE'S CORNER."

"Almost done?" Adam Joshua's mother asked, going by the door and finding Adam Joshua sitting in the middle of the piles playing marbles.

"Almost," said Adam Joshua, putting all of his marbles in a sock he found under the bed, and then putting the sock back under there.

Behind his dresser, Adam Joshua found his fishing pole with an old worm still on it. He took the worm off and climbed up on his bed.

"Fore!" yelled Adam Joshua, and he cast with his fishing pole. The line went up and over his hanging light, and around the back of his rocking chair, and the hook caught at the top of his curtains.

"Hole-in-one," said Adam Joshua, climbing down and leaning the pole against the wall.

He looked at the clock.

"Fifteen minutes," he said.

George went by the door and stopped, and backed up, and came in to help.

"Okay," Adam Joshua told George. "You can help, but we've got to get busy. We've only got fifteen minutes."

While Adam Joshua got busy making new piles out of old ones, George unmade them.

While Adam Joshua got busy stacking things up, George got busy unstacking them.

While Adam Joshua got busier, George got into more trouble.

"Enough help," said Adam Joshua, untangling George from a tangle of twine. "Stay there," said Adam Joshua, putting George up on the bed and out of the way.

"I mean it!" yelled Adam Joshua as he started to get down.

Adam Joshua pushed a pile of building bricks across the room to a pile of comic books. Then he pushed the brick and comic book piles over and dumped the dinosaur pile on top. Adam Joshua kept pushing until he had an enormous pile made up of piles and then he pushed it all into the closet and pushed to get the door shut.

George jumped off the bed, and crawled

under the bed, and crawled back out again with the sock in his mouth. He gave the sock a shake, and marbles rolled all over the floor.

The alarm clock went off.

"Here I am," said Nelson.

Nelson brought two suitcases, a sleeping bag, and his special pillow.

"Allergies," said Nelson, dumping everything on Adam Joshua's bed.

"This room's a mess," said Nelson, looking around the room that Adam Joshua had just finished cleaning.

"Bring a broom," said Nelson, bending down to pick up marbles.

Nelson swept the floor, and then he swept part of it again, and he put his sleeping bag down here.

He unpacked his suitcases. He unpacked pajamas, and his robe, and his slippers. He unpacked his toothbrush, and his hairbrush, and some toothpaste. Nelson unpacked a flashlight, and a book about fish, a soccer ball, and his Armand's Legion of Space Spies. He unpacked boots, the one-eyed, one-armed, no-legged teddy bear Adam Joshua had let him borrow again, and his tie.

"I always wear a tie for supper," said Nelson.

Nelson unpacked three tuna and peanut

125

butter sandwiches, and four oatmeal cookies.

"Might not like supper," he said.

"I brought you presents, Adam Joshua," said Nelson. He unpacked a broken stick from an old drum set, and the ladder from a missing fire truck.

"Why, thank you very much," said Adam Joshua.

"I knew you'd love them, Adam Joshua," said Nelson, handing him half a licked lollipop too.

When he was finished with unpacking, Nelson walked over to Adam Joshua's closet to put his suitcases away. Adam Joshua's pile of piles fell out all over him the minute he opened the door.

"Adam Joshua!" yelled Nelson, shaking a dinosaur off his foot. "This is no way to treat a friend!"

———

Adam Joshua and Nelson played space spies and real spies, and Adam Joshua let Nelson be the hero every time.

"Ow, ugh!" Adam Joshua would yell when

he got hit. "You were too smart for me!" he'd say, groaning and dying a long, slow death.

"Don't worry about it, Adam Joshua," said Nelson.

Adam Joshua and Nelson played soccer, and they played "Go Fish," because it was Nelson's favorite game, and they sat on Adam Joshua's bed telling jokes.

"Knock, knock," said Adam Joshua.

"I've already heard that one," said Nelson.

"Pick a card," said Nelson. "Any card."

"Nelson," Adam Joshua told him, "you've only got two cards."

"Adam Joshua," said Nelson, shuffling them, "it's a lot harder trick this way than with just one."

Nelson wore his tie to supper. "And I like it fine," he whispered to Adam Joshua as he passed his plate for seconds.

After supper they watched TV.

"That's not the show I watch, Adam Joshua," Nelson said, polite.

"It's the show I always watch," Adam Joshua said, polite.

"The superhero on this show is very dumb, Adam Joshua," said Nelson, not so polite.

"I think he's terrific," said Adam Joshua, not polite at all.

"I really hate this show!" Nelson said, yelling.

"It's my very favorite one!" Adam Joshua yelled back.

"You went through a big fight not long ago," Adam Joshua's father said, coming in to see what all the yelling was about. "Do you really want to start it again?"

"We'll watch whatever you want," Adam Joshua told Nelson, polite again.

"Don't bother; I hate TV anyway," said Nelson.

————

Adam Joshua let Nelson choose a game because Nelson was a guest.

They played checkers, and Adam Joshua let Nelson win because Nelson was a guest.

"Don't worry about it, Adam Joshua," Nelson said. "We'll play more on other days, and I'll teach you to be as good as me."

"I can tell you a ghost story," said Adam Joshua.

"Boring," said Nelson. "But you'll love this," he said, getting out his book on fish.

"I can make popcorn," said Adam Joshua.

"Hate popcorn," said Nelson. "But you'll love these," he said, getting out his tuna fish and peanut butter sandwiches.

Nelson took a bath with his boots on.

"Nelson," Adam Joshua told him, "I can't believe it. You can't take a bath that way. Your boots will get full of water and pull you to the bottom. You'll drown."

"Can't go far to the bottom in a bathtub," said Nelson. "And I never take a bath without my boots."

"Your feet never get clean!" Adam Joshua yelled.

"They last longer that way!" Nelson yelled back.

———

Adam Joshua sat down outside the bathroom door to wait while Nelson finished his bath. George came and sat beside him to wait too.

"I can't take it," Adam Joshua told George. "Everything Nelson is doing is driving me crazy."

George didn't say anything.

"I know how you feel," Adam Joshua told George. "I know you like him, and I know he's not perfect. But he doesn't have to be so crazy. He could just be ordinary."

Nelson went by.

"Bathtub's yours, Adam Joshua," said Nelson. "You can borrow my boots if you'd like."

"I'd settle for ordinary anytime," Adam Joshua told George.

———

"Would you rather have the bed?" Adam Joshua asked Nelson, polite.

"Why, the floor will be fine, Adam Joshua," said Nelson, getting into his sleeping bag.

"Lights on or off?" Adam Joshua asked Nelson, polite.

"Well, off would be fine," said Nelson.

Adam Joshua turned off the light. Everything was dark. Everything got quiet.

"I'm not sleepy," said Nelson.

It was great being in the dark with Nelson. Adam Joshua told Nelson stories, and Nelson told Adam Joshua jokes. They told each other secrets, and they promised not to tell the secrets, and Nelson never laughed once about the things Adam Joshua told him. Adam Joshua loved George, but it was nice to talk to some-body at night who could answer back.

Adam Joshua had been waiting for a long time for Nelson to say something about Super-man, but Nelson never had. Adam Joshua didn't think it would hurt to ask.

"Nelson," he said, "did you ever decide that you believed in Superman?"

Nelson was quiet in the dark for a long time.

"Never heard of him," he finally said.

Just as Adam Joshua and Nelson were fall-ing asleep, George came trotting into the room, and bounced and climbed until he got to his place on top of Adam Joshua's bed.

Nelson's flashlight went on.

"He can't stay here!" Nelson yelled, point-ing his flashlight at George.

"I won't have it!" he yelled, waving his flash-light all around.

"It's his room too," said Adam Joshua, get-ting out of bed and turning on the light, and patting George on the head so he wouldn't be afraid of Nelson.

"George should get to say if you stay!" Adam Joshua told Nelson. He found chalk and he took it and drew a circle around his bed.

"Stay inside, George," he said. "Be polite."

Adam Joshua drew a circle on the floor around Nelson's sleeping bag.

"Stay inside, Nelson," he said.

"Adam Joshua!" yelled Nelson. "What do you think you're doing?"

"Fair's fair," said Adam Joshua, turning out the light and getting back into bed.

Everything was dark. Everything got quiet.

George jumped off the bed, dragging Fred along.

Nelson's flashlight went on.

"Your dog's trying to eat me!" Nelson yelled. "He's licking my feet!"

"If you didn't take baths with your boots on," Adam Joshua hollered back, "your feet would be cleaner and he wouldn't think he had to wash them."

"Get him off me and move it!" Nelson yelled.

Adam Joshua got out of bed, and got George, and took George back to bed with him.

"Okay, George," sighed Adam Joshua, settling George down again. George went right to sleep.

"And take this with you," Nelson yelled, throwing George's blanket, Fred. "It smells just terrible, Adam Joshua."

"My dog likes things to smell that way, Nelson," said Adam Joshua. "Must be why he likes your feet."

George stayed asleep. Nelson went to sleep.

"And about time," said Adam Joshua, going to sleep himself.

The dark and quiet stayed there for a while.

Then Nelson let out a scream.

"I thought it was a spider, Adam Joshua," said Nelson, after the light was back on and everyone was back up.

"It wasn't a spider, it was a string on the sleeping bag," Nelson said. "But I thought it was a spider.

"Adam Joshua," said Nelson, lying down, "ever since Cynthia, I've had a lot of problems about spiders."

Adam Joshua could understand that.

"Don't you worry, Nelson," he said, tucking everyone back in. "We're here if you need us," he yawned.

This time Adam Joshua didn't even try to go to sleep. He stayed wide awake and waited.

In a few minutes, Nelson's flashlight went on.

"I'll be right back, Adam Joshua," said Nelson, crawling out of his sleeping bag, and walking out of the room.

Adam Joshua stayed awake and waited.

Nelson didn't come back.

"I'll be right back, George," Adam Joshua said.

He got out of bed and looked all over the upstairs for Nelson.

Nelson wasn't there.

Adam Joshua went downstairs in the dark to look for Nelson.

He wasn't there either.

Adam Joshua sat down at the kitchen table to think about things. The kitchen door opened

and Nelson came through it with his flashlight in his mouth, and a bowl in his arms.

"My fish, Adam Joshua," said Nelson. "I can't sleep without them.

"And my fish, Adam Joshua," said Nelson, going up the stairs with fish water sloshing along behind him, "can't sleep without me.

"Good night now," said Nelson, crawling back into his sleeping bag with his fishbowl on the floor beside him.

"Good night, Nelson," Adam Joshua muttered, crawling back into bed with George.

George licked Adam Joshua on the nose, and curled up on his stomach.

Then he saw the fish.

George jumped off the bed and barked. He put his nose in the fishbowl, and his paw in the fishbowl, and howled.

Nelson howled along.

"Your dog's eating my fish!" he howled.

"My dog wouldn't want your fish!" Adam Joshua shouted. "My dog hates fish!" he yelled. "Just like me," he hollered. "Exactly like me!"

"Got a problem?" asked Adam Joshua's father, standing in the doorway with half his robe on, and Adam Joshua's mother coming along behind him.

"His dog!" yelled Nelson.

"His fish!" yelled Adam Joshua.

In the next room, Amanda Jane woke up and started yelling too.

"I'll handle it," Adam Joshua told his parents, sending them back to bed. "Don't you worry about a thing. It's my problem.

"It's my friend," he said, making Nelson get

in the bed, and putting his fishbowl high up on the dresser.

"It's my dog," said Adam Joshua, giving George a tickle on his tummy, and a kiss on the nose to stop his howling, and pushing him down to the end of the sleeping bag.

"It's my sister," Adam Joshua said, going into Amanda Jane's room and carrying her back to his.

"You might as well be in here too," he told her. "Everybody else is."

Adam Joshua crawled down inside Nelson's sleeping bag with Amanda Jane. George crawled up to meet them.

"Why, this is much better, Adam Joshua," said Nelson in the dark. "We should have thought of this sooner," he said.

"Not another word, Nelson," said Adam Joshua. "Just don't say a thing."

George curled up on top of Adam Joshua, and Adam Joshua patted him. Amanda Jane curled up beside Adam Joshua, and Adam Joshua rocked her. George's blanket, Fred, came sailing through the air in the dark and

landed right on top of Adam Joshua's head, but Nelson never said a word.

———

"It was nice to have you come," Adam Joshua told Nelson after breakfast.

"Well, it was nice of you to ask me," said Nelson, putting suitcases under his arms, and picking up his fishbowl, and leaning over to get his pillow with his teeth.

"I hope you'll come again soon," Adam Joshua called after Nelson, polite.

"Mmmph, mmmph!" Nelson called back through a mouthful of pillow, as he went, sloshing fish water along behind him.

———

In Adam Joshua's room, George was curled up on the bed, sound asleep.

"I know how you feel," said Adam Joshua, getting ready to curl up too.

On Adam Joshua's dresser was Adam Joshua's toothbrush glass.

It had a fish in it.

"FOR YOU, ADAM JOSHUA," a note beside the glass said. "**BECAUSE YOU'RE MY BEST FRIEND, AND BECAUSE I LIKE YOU, AND BECAUSE YOU UNDERSTAND.**"

Adam Joshua looked at the fish for a long time, and then he went over and curled up beside George.

George rolled over, and crawled up on Adam Joshua's stomach without ever opening an eye. "I don't understand a thing about you, Nelson," said Adam Joshua.

"But I like you anyway," he said, falling asleep too.

ABOUT THE AUTHOR

Janice Lee Smith's THE KID NEXT DOOR AND OTHER HEADACHES *continues the humorous adventures of Adam Joshua, the spunky hero she first introduced in* THE MONSTER IN THE THIRD DRESSER DRAWER.

Ms. Smith was graduated with high honors from Douglass College of Rutgers University in New Jersey, and received the Edna Herzburg Award for Essay. She lives with her husband, James, and their two children, Bryan and Jaymi, in Noblesville, Indiana.

ABOUT THE ARTIST

Dick Gackenbach, the illustrator of Janice Lee Smith's first collection of Adam Joshua stories, THE MONSTER IN THE THIRD DRESSER DRAWER, *is also the author/illustrator of over a score of books of his own. Some of his most recent titles are* MCGOOGAN MOVES THE MIGHTY ROCK; MR. WINK AND HIS SHADOW, NED; *and* THE DOG AND THE DEEP DARK WOODS.

Mr. Gackenbach lives in Washington Depot, Connecticut.

Set in 12 pt. Baskerville
Composed by NK Graphics
HarperCollins Publishers